Developing Reader titles are ideal
using their phonics knowledge and
with only a little help. Frequently re
fluency and confidence.

Special features:

Short, simple sentences

Peppa is going to a sleepover
at Zoe Zebra's house.

"Hello, Peppa!" says Zoe.

Frequent
repetition of
main story words
and phrases

Careful match
between story
and pictures

Oh dear! The noise has
woken Daddy Zebra up!

"We are just having a story,
Daddy," says Zoe.

Daddy Zebra joins in with
the story.

Large, clear
type

26

27

Ladybird

Educational Consultants: Geraldine Taylor and James Clements
Book Banding Consultant: Kate Ruttle

LADYBIRD BOOKS
UK | USA | Canada | Ireland | Australia
India | New Zealand | South Africa

Ladybird Books is part of the Penguin Random House group of companies
whose addresses can be found at global.penguinrandomhouse.com.

www.penguin.co.uk   www.puffin.co.uk   www.ladybird.co.uk

Text adapted from *Peppa Pig: Peppa's First Sleepover* first published by Ladybird Books Ltd 2012
Read It Yourself edition first published by Ladybird Books Ltd 2016
This edition published 2024
001

Licensed by

Printed in China

The authorized representative in the EEA is Penguin Random House Ireland,
Morrison Chambers, 32 Nassau Street, Dublin D02 YH68

A CIP catalogue record for this book is available from the British Library

ISBN: 978-0-241-56539-1

All correspondence to:
Ladybird Books
Penguin Random House Children's
One Embassy Gardens, 8 Viaduct Gardens, London SW11 7BW

MIX
Paper from
responsible sources
FSC® C018179

First Sleepover

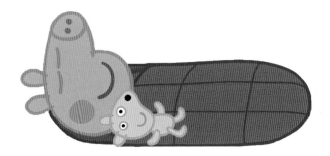

Adapted by Ellen Philpott

Peppa is going to a sleepover
at Zoe Zebra's house.

"Hello, Peppa!" says Zoe.

7

Rebecca Rabbit,
Suzy Sheep and
Emily Elephant are
at Zoe's house, too.

Everyone says hello
to Peppa.

"Be very quiet, girls!"
says Mummy Zebra.
"Don't wake Daddy Zebra up.
He has to go to work in
the morning."

"Can we join in with the sleepover?" say Zoe's little sisters.

Zoe does not want them to.

"You are too little," she says.

13

Oh no! Zoe's little sisters are crying! They want to be at the sleepover, too.

"Can they join in?" says Rebecca Rabbit.

Zoe says her sisters can
join in, so then they
stop crying.

"What do you do at a sleepover?" says Suzy Sheep.

"We will play a song on the piano," says Zoe.

Emily Elephant joins in. Then Peppa joins in.

Everyone plays on
the piano.

Oh no! Mummy Zebra
has woken up.

"Be quiet! Stop playing!"
says Mummy Zebra.
"Don't wake Daddy Zebra up!
He has to go to work in
the morning."

"What are we going to do now?"
says Peppa.

"We will have a midnight feast!"
says Zoe.

Everyone wants to have
a midnight feast.

"Be quiet! Don't make so much noise," says Zoe.

They go and have a midnight feast.

"Be quiet, girls!"
says Mummy Zebra.
"Daddy Zebra has to go
to work in the morning.
Just have a quiet
story now."

Everyone joins in with
the story. They are not
very quiet.

Oh no! The noise has woken Daddy Zebra up!

"We are just having a story, Daddy," says Zoe.

Daddy Zebra joins in with
the story.

Then Daddy Zebra plays them a song on the piano.

The quiet song makes everyone go to sleep!

How much do you remember about the story of *Peppa Pig: First Sleepover*? Answer these questions and find out!

- Whose house is Peppa going to?

- Which instrument does Zoe play a song on?

- What does Daddy Zebra do to help everyone go to sleep?

- Who wants to be at the sleepover, too?